NATURAL HISTORY

NATURAL HISTORY

BY

M. B. GOFFSTEIN

FARRAR · STRAUS · GIROUX / New York

Copyright © 1979 by **M. B. Goffstein**   /   All rights reserved

Library of Congress catalog card number: 79-7318

Published simultaneously in Canada by McGraw-Hill Ryerson Ltd., Toronto

Color separations by Offset Separations Corp.

Printed in the United States of America by Eastern Press, Inc.

Bound by A. Horowitz and Son

Designed by Cynthia Krupat   /   First edition, 1979

TO BARLA

Our planet is a lively ball
in the universe.

Oceans move ceaselessly,
and below, in the deep,

fish swim, mollusks hop,
and plants wave silently.

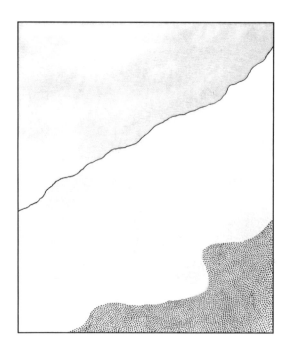

Tiny grains of sand
keep the powerful waters
from flooding lands

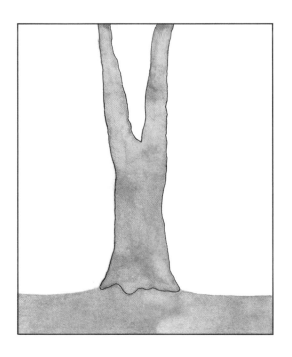

where trees grow skyward.

It looks so peaceful
from afar.

But little puffs of smoke
erupt
where men are fighting,

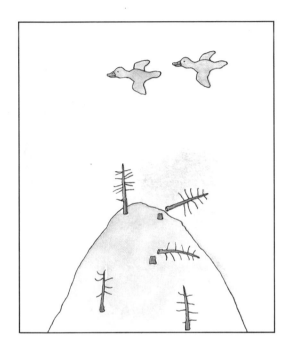

or shooting ducks
down from the sky,
or breaking mountains.

Homeless dogs and cats
are scared and lonely.

Old people look in garbage
hopefully,

though we have riches
we are born to share.

Low trees hold fruit

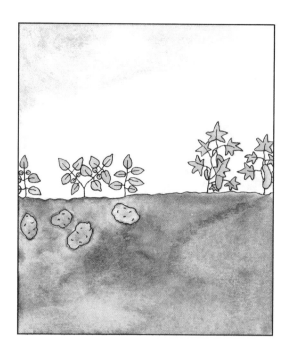

and vegetables lie warmly
in the dirt
or hide on vines.

Waves of wheat and corn
shimmer in the sun.
They are made for people.

They're made for cows
who nurse their calves.

They're made for gray wolves
with their pups.

They're made for ducks
and singing birds and snakes
and little minks.

Every living creature
is our brother and our sister,

dearer than the jewels
at the center of the earth.

So let us be
like tiny grains of sand,

and protect all life
from fear and suffering!

Then, when the stars shine,
we can sleep in peace,

with the moon
as our quiet night-light.